if you Hold a seed

by Elly MacKay

RP|KIDS
PHILADELPHIA • LONDON

To my mother,
who finds magic in the smallest of places.

To my father,
who showed me the potential of a tiny seed. . . .

Books published by Running Press are available at special discounts for bulk purchases in the United States
by corporations, institutions, and other organizations. For more information, please contact the Special Markets
Department at the Perseus Books Group, 2300 Chestnut Street, Suite 200, Philadelphia, PA 19103,
or call (800) 810-4145, ext. 5000, or e-mail special.markets@perseusbooks.com.

ISBN 978-0-7624-4721-3

Library of Congress Control Number: 2012947641

9 8 7 6 5 4 3 2 1
Digit on the right indicates the number of this printing

Designed by Frances J. Soo Ping Chow
Edited by Marlo Scrimizzi
Typography: Matchbook, Mr. Moustache, and Sans Serif

Published by Running Press Kids
An Imprint of Running Press Book Publishers
A Member of the Perseus Books Group
2300 Chestnut Street
Philadelphia, PA 19103-4371

Visit us on the web!
www.runningpress.com

If you hold a seed,
And make a wish,
And plant it in the ground...

Something magical can happen.

And if there is some sun . . .

And some rain . . .
It will begin to sprout.

And if you wait . . .

And wait . . .

You will see some little buds,
And tender leaves.

When summer comes,
There might be a bee...

...Or perhaps a butterfly.

And they will spread some magic.

But when autumn comes...

All its leaves will fall.

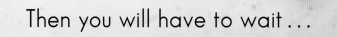
Then you will have to wait . . .

Through all the winter days.

Until spring!

The tree will grow,
With buds of gold and green.

Birds will come to perch,
Perhaps to sing.

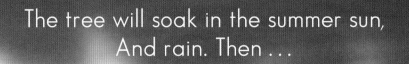
The tree will soak in the summer sun,
And rain. Then . . .

When autumn comes again,
It will lean into the wind.

And if you wait and wait . . .

Season by season,
Year by year...

That tree will grow SO LARGE
It will hold you.

And . . .

If you wait some more, one day,
Your wish...

Will come true.